Hundreds upon hundreds of years ago, in a place called Flower Fruit Mountain, there was a remarkable little kingdom of monkeys. And by far the most remarkable thing about this kingdom was its king, who was known simply as Monkey King...

千百年前，有一個地方叫做花果山。
花果山上有一個很有名的猴子國，
猴子國最了不起的，就是它的國王
—美猴王…

To the two loveliest boys
in the world, Melvin and
Darren, and the culture
that has nurtured me.
— D. C.

In memory of Shuching,
my beloved wife.
— W. M.

English and Chinese texts copyright © 2001, Debby Chen
Illustrations copyright © 2001, Wenhai Ma
English editing: Frank Araujo and William Mersereau

Published in the United States of America by
Pan Asian Publications (USA) Inc.
29564 Union City Boulevard, Union City, CA 94587
Tel. (510) 475-1185   Fax (510) 475-1489

Published in Canada by
Pan Asian Publications Inc.
110 Silver Star Boulevard, Unit 109
Scarborough, Ontario M1V-5A2

ISBN 1-57227-070-5
Library of Congress Catalog Card Number: 00-107317

Cover design: Yudi Sewraj
Editorial and production assistance: Art & Publishing Consultants

Printed in China by the South China Printing Co. Ltd.

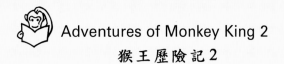
MONKEY KING
wreaks havoc in
HEAVEN

美猴王大鬧天宮

Retold by Debby Chen • Illustrated by Wenhai Ma

English / Chinese

Pan Asian Publications

Monkey King had been born from a magic stone and had learned many powerful, mystical arts. His little monkey subjects loved him dearly – especially after he rescued them from some demons! He now decided that they had to learn to defend themselves. He trained a few thousand of them, and soon he had a very strong little army.

Monkey King was proud of his warriors, but something was still missing. "I need a royal weapon!" he declared. "It must show everyone what a great king I am!" An old monkey came forward and said that the Dragon King had a strange and powerful iron wand. Monkey King was delighted – he had always wanted to visit the old dragon's undersea palace.

美猴王是從仙石中生出來的，他會很多神奇的法術和武功。有一回美猴王打敗混世魔王，救出許多小猴子，從此大家更敬愛他了。爲了訓練衆猴自衛，美猴王教小猴子們耍槍練劍，很快地就組成了一支武藝高強的猴子軍。

美猴王很滿意猴子兵的表現，但他還是不滿足。有一天他說：「我需要一件最好的武器，好讓所有的人知道我美猴王有多了不起！」這時，一隻老猴子站出來對他說：「東海龍王有一支神奇的鐵棒！」美猴王聽了很高興，因爲他一直想去海底的龍宮看看呢！

Monkey King said some magic words and flew on a cloud to the sea. He skimmed across the waves and then plunged down, down to the Dragon King's palace. He marched up to the old king, saying, "I'm Monkey King. I've heard you have a powerful wand. Bring it to me!"

The Dragon King's eyes narrowed. "I've no such thing!" he hissed. Monkey King sneered, "Don't try to hide anything from me!" He pulled on the old dragon's whiskers. Wise Dragon King sensed right away that he could not match Monkey King's power in a battle, so he did not argue further. He swallowed hard and said, "All right, follow me...but I'm sure even *you* can't lift it!"

美猴王唸了幾句咒語，只見他騰雲駕霧、穿浪下海，一下
子就到了龍宮。他雄赳赳、氣昂昂地走到龍王面前說：「
我是美猴王，聽說你有一支神奇的鐵棒，快拿出來給我瞧
瞧！」

龍王雙眼一瞪：「我没有這樣的東西！」美猴王冷笑說：
「少騙我！」順手一把抓住老龍王的鬍鬚。聰明的龍王知
道自己鬥不過美猴王，只好嘆口氣說：「也罷，跟我來！
不過，我相信連你也抬不動它！」

He led Monkey King into a dark forest of seaweed. There they found a glowing metal pillar. "This has been here for over a million years. Some say the gods used it when they built the starry night sky. It's fantastically heavy – no one has ever been able to lift it."

"Let *me* see about that!" Monkey exclaimed. He grabbed the rod and began pulling and twisting it. The ground crackled, sparks flew, and the ancient iron slipped free. On it was written,

Ruyi the golden rod which weighs 36,000 kilos

Monkey King frowned, "What does Ruyi mean?" Dragon King explained that Ruyi is the staff that grows or shrinks as its master wishes. "Hooray!" cried Monkey King, "Now I can lead the Monkey Army!"

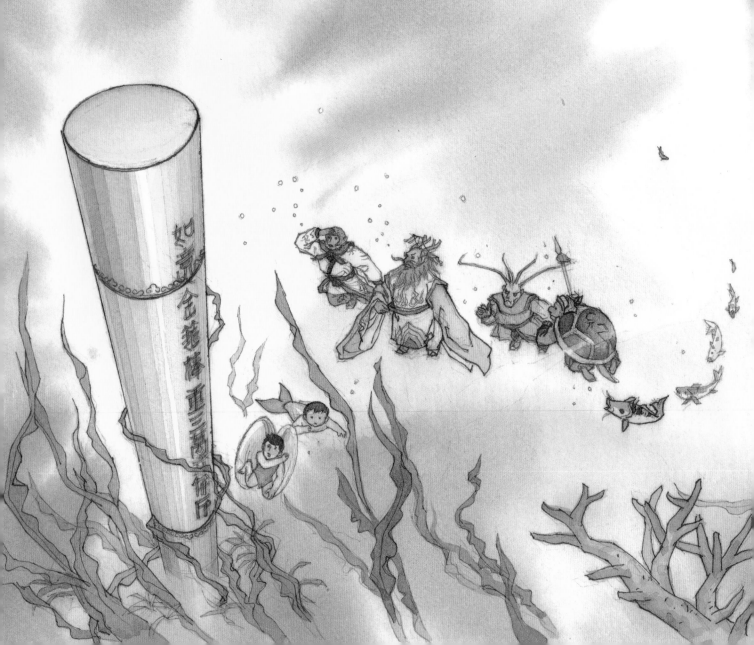

老龍王帶著美猴王來到黑漆漆的海藻叢裏，在那兒，他們看到一支閃閃發光的鐵柱子。龍王說：「這支鐵柱子插在海底已經一百多萬年了，據說眾神在開天闢地的時候，曾經用它造了閃爍的星空。這鐵柱奇重無比，從來沒有人能夠搬得動它。」

「讓我試試！」美猴王抱著鐵柱子前後搖動了幾下。忽然地裂開了，火花四濺，這支古老的鐵柱子就這樣輕而易舉地被他拔了起來。只見鐵柱上刻著一行字：

如意金箍棒，重三萬六千公斤

美猴王皺起眉頭問：「如意是什麼意思？」龍王說「如意」是指鐵柱可隨主人之意伸長或縮短。「太好了！」美猴王叫道：「現在我可以帶兵打仗了！」

Dragon King was relieved to see Monkey King preparing to leave. But before going, the naughty monkey helped himself to some of the Dragon's finest clothes – including a red-gold cap made of phoenix feathers.

Then, with a quick back flip, Monkey soared home. His little monkey soldiers stared in awe as their king showed them the glowing metal rod. "Shrink!" he shouted. Ruyi shrank to the size of a toothpick. Then he shouted, "Now, GROW!" Ruyi grew and grew. The ground shook as Monkey grew with it and his laughter rang through the valleys. "Now we are invincible!" he roared.

眼見美猴王就要離開了，老龍王終於鬆了一口氣。沒想到調皮的美猴王又折回來，在龍宮裏翻箱倒櫃，把龍王最漂亮的衣服和一套珍貴的鳳翅金冠拿走了。

一個翻身，美猴王又回到花果山。他穿上新衣服，拿出金箍棒在眾猴面前耍弄。小猴子看得目瞪眼呆、哇哇叫好。「變小！」美猴王大喊，金箍棒變成一支小牙籤；「變長！」金箍棒越變越長，美猴王也越長越高，連他腳下的地都動搖了。「現在我們是天下無敵了！」他得意地大笑，笑聲在山谷裡迴響。

Meanwhile, far above in the Heavenly Palace, the Dragon King had made a formal complaint about Monkey King before the Jade Emperor. The ruler of Heaven thought of a plan to teach Monkey King some manners. He sent a messenger down to Earth to invite the monkey to Heaven. "How wonderful!" cried Monkey King. "I've always wanted to see whether Heaven is as great as they say!" And before long, Monkey King was strolling through the inner court of the Heavenly Palace. He waved to the Jade Emperor on his throne. "Hello there! What can I do for you?" he asked casually.

就在這時，東海龍王來到天宮，把美猴王做的壞事一五一十說給玉皇大帝
聽。玉皇大帝想出一個管教美猴王的妙計，於是派遣使者去請美猴王來天
宮。

「好極了！我一直想去天宮看看那兒是否像人們說的那麼了不得！」才說
完，美猴王一個翻身就到了天宮。他向坐在龍椅上的玉皇大帝招招手，毫
不在乎地說：「嗨！你找我來做什麼？」

The Jade Emperor frowned, but then he smiled. "Monkey King of Flower Fruit Mountain," he said in a deep voice, "I appoint you my new Master of the Imperial Stables. You shall tend to the celestial horses." Now Monkey knew that very few people from Earth are ever promoted to a post in Heaven, so he felt very proud of himself.

Monkey worked hard at his new job, and the horses seemed to like him as their caretaker. But one day he heard two guards laughing at him. "What are you laughing at?" Monkey King demanded.

"On Earth, you bragged of your greatness," the guard snickered, "but here in Heaven, you clean dung from our stables! Ha! Ha!" Monkey King's eyes blazed, as he sensed the truth of the words. "Nobody makes a fool of me!" he said to himself. "I'll get that crafty Jade Emperor!" He threw open the stables and chased away the horses. And then with a double flip, he flew home. He ordered his monkeys to raise a banner on the top of Flower Fruit Mountain that read:

Monkey King the Sage Is Equal to Any in Heaven!

玉皇大帝覺得美猴王很沒禮貌，不過他還是和氣地笑著說：
「花果山來的美猴王，我封你爲弼馬溫，照顧天馬。」美猴
王知道很少有人能在天庭做官，因此他覺得很光榮，馬上就
答應了。

美猴王努力工作，馬兒也很喜歡他。不過有一天，他看到兩
個小管理員在旁邊偷笑。「你們笑什麼？」他生氣地問。

「哈！哈！你說天下你最大，可是到了天上，你卻在馬房裏
清馬糞！」美猴王發現自己上當了，氣得雙眼冒火。他破口
大叫：「狡猾的玉皇大帝膽敢愚弄我，我一定要他好看！」
他一腳踢開馬房，把所有的馬匹都趕走了。然後連翻兩個筋
斗又回到了花果山。他命令小猴子在山頂上立起一面大旗，
旗上寫著：

齊天大聖

The Jade Emperor was genuinely angry with Monkey King–first for turning
his horses loose, and now for daring to declare himself equal to any immortal
in Heaven. The Emperor sent his best warrior, the three-headed Prince Nazha,
to defeat Monkey King.

Monkey King stood his ground and fought Prince Nazha brilliantly for
two days and nights. Finally he split himself into two. One monkey fought Nazha
face to face while the other jumped on him from behind.

玉皇大帝眞的動怒了一美猴王不僅趕走他的馬，還敢稱自己是齊天大聖。
於是，他派最厲害的戰士，可變出三頭六臂的哪吒太子去捉拿美猴王。

美猴王挺身迎戰。他和哪吒激戰了兩天兩夜，最後他使出分身術，變出另
一個美猴王；一個美猴王和哪吒迎面對打，另一個美猴王從哪吒的背後偷
擊。

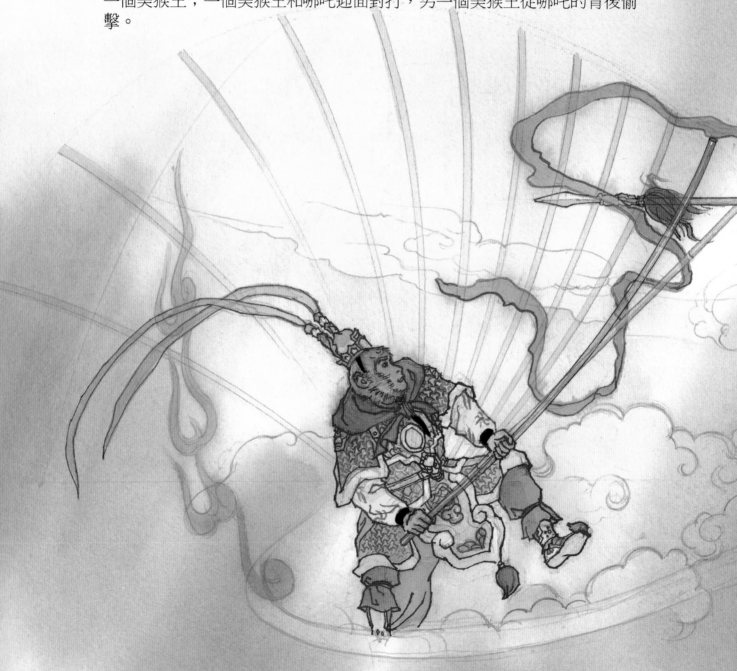

Prince Nazha then took a blow from Ruyi that could have flattened a mountain. More ashamed than hurt, Nazha fled back to Heaven.

哪吒太子被金箍棒像泰山壓頂似地重重地打了一下，痛得他又羞又怒，狼狽地逃回天宮。

Jade Emperor was hopping with anger when he learned of Prince Nazha's defeat. "That monkey must be destroyed! Call up my Heavenly Army!" But his trusted advisor, White-Gold Star, was worried. "Your Majesty, it would look bad if more of our fine warriors were humiliated by an earthly monkey. The best battles are those we don't fight. Let me talk to him. I'll make him the Guardian of the Sacred Orchards. It's an important but boring job, so it will teach him patience and responsibility."

Calming himself, the Jade Emperor agreed to his advisor's plan. Sure enough, with some flattering words and promises of treats and comforts, Monkey King happily accepted the job in the fragrant celestial orchard.

Now, in one part of the orchard there grew sacred peach trees whose juicy fruit ripened only once every thousand years. Whoever ate one of these peaches became immortal. Monkey King soon found some ripe peaches and, of course, he ate each and every one. With a full tummy, he then shrank to the size of a worm and took a nap on a leafy branch. Before long, seven fairy maids appeared.

看到哪吒太子倉皇逃回，玉皇大帝氣得跳腳：「該死的猴子，天兵天將備戰！」可是，德高望重的太白金星不贊成這樣做，他說：「陛下，如果我們又輸給那隻土猴子，不是很沒面子嗎？兵家常說最好的戰術是不戰而屈人之兵。為何不召他來管蟠桃園？他每天抓蟲除草，慢慢會培養出耐心和責任感。」

玉皇大帝的氣稍平了以後，就再派太白金星到花果山。美猴王聽了太白金星的一番好話，想到有吃有喝，又可住在香氣四溢的蟠桃園，就高高興興地跟他回到天宮。

蟠桃園中種有神奇的桃樹，它的果子幾千年才成熟一次，誰吃了果子就可以長生不老。美猴王很快地就找到了那些成熟的桃子，不用說，一個個桃子都被他吃進肚子裏去了。吃飽後，他就把自己變得像小蟲一樣小，躺在樹枝上呼呼大睡。不久，七仙女來到蟠桃園。

The maidens had been sent to pick the ripe peaches, but, seeing only green fruit, they burst into tears. Monkey King awoke with a start, shouting, "Hey! Who's crying?"

"Orchard Guardian, help us!" cried the eldest maiden. "Someone has taken the ripe peaches we were supposed to pick for Her Majesty's birthday party!" Monkey King jumped up. "A birthday party? Now why wasn't I invited?" The fairies then saw peach pits scattered nearby. But before they could cry out, Monkey King made a magic sign and the maids froze like statues of marble. "Now, let's find that party!" he said, setting off for the Heavenly Palace.

In the palace cookhouse, Monkey King smelled delicious buns baking. These special buns had magic spices that made whoever ate them impervious to both fire and pain. Monkey King plucked hairs from his head and changed them into mosquitoes that bit the bakers and made them fall asleep on the spot. The monkey gobbled up all the magic buns.

七仙女是來採仙桃給王母娘娘過生日的。可是，成熟的紅仙桃在哪裡呢？園內只有青綠的生桃子，她們急得哭了。美猴王被哭聲吵醒，很不耐煩地說：「誰在哭啊？」

「管桃園的公公，求求您幫個忙！」大仙女哭著說：「有人把紅仙桃摘走了，那是王母娘娘壽宴上要吃的啊！」「壽宴？怎麼沒請我？」美猴王氣得跳起來。這時仙女們看到地上散落的桃渣，還來不及叫，一個個都被美猴王用定身術定在原地。「好了，現在我要去找擺壽宴的地方。」說完後他一溜煙似地往天宮去。

天宮的廚房裏飄出陣陣餅香，美猴王好想吃啊！這些仙餅是要給天神天將吃的，吃了以後不怕水淹，也不怕火烤。美猴王從頭上拔下一些毛，「呼」的一吹，毛都變成瞌睡蟲，這些瞌睡蟲一叮到廚師，他們馬上就呼呼大睡，美猴王便趁機把仙餅吃個精光。

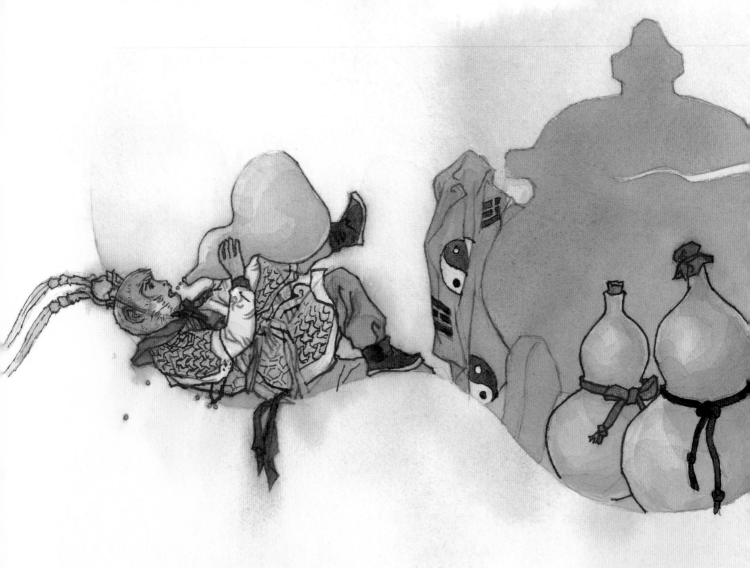

Inside the palace, Monkey King found jugs of the Emperor's favorite drink –
a potion made of rubies and jade that gave endless youth. Monkey King drank
deeply, emptying several jugs. But White-Gold Star soon found the empty jugs
and sounded the alarm. "Someone has raided the Emperor's potion!" His cries
awoke the bakers, who shouted, "Someone has eaten the Magic Sweet Buns!"
Their cries awoke the fairy maids. "Help! Help! The Sacred Peaches have been
stolen!" The Heavenly Palace was now in a terrible panic. Monkey King, with
his belly full of heavenly food and drink, stole away on a cloud back to Flower
Fruit Mountain.

Later, it was White-Gold Star's turn to be boiling angry. "Your Majesty!
That horrid ape ruined the Empress' party. He ate the sacred peaches, stuffed
himself with magic buns, and drank many jugs of your favorite potion!"
Jade Emperor shook his head in disbelief, then said, "I have instructed Erlang,
my finest general, to lead the Heavenly Army against Monkey King."

走啊走，美猴王又找到一樣好東西－玉皇大帝最喜愛的金玉仙露，
聽說喝了它可以長生不老。就在美猴王大喝特喝的時候，太白金星
來了，他大驚：「有人偷喝了仙露！」這麼一喊，廚師們都醒了，
他們大叫：「有人偷吃了仙餅！」接著七仙女也被嚇醒了，她們大
哭：「不好了！不好了！有人偷吃了仙桃！」天宮裡亂成一團，而
闖禍的美猴王呢？他摸著脹得鼓鼓的肚子，偷偷溜回花果山去了。

這回輪到太白金星大發雷霆了：「陛下！那隻可惡的
猴子偷吃了仙桃、仙餅和仙露，把王母娘娘的壽宴搞
得一團糟！」玉皇大帝不敢相信地搖搖頭說：「好！
我這就派我最神勇的天將－二郎神帶領天兵天將去捉
拿那妖猴。」

General Erlang flew down on his giant eagle to Flower Fruit Mountain as the Heavenly Army fought the Monkey Army. Erlang challenged Monkey King to single combat. Armed with Ruyi, Monkey King clashed with Erlang. The mountains, the seas, even the sun, moon, and stars all shook with each dreadful blow. Erlang was the most powerful opponent Monkey King had ever faced. The Monkey Army soon retreated to Water Curtain Cave, their hideout behind a waterfall. "Surrender now!" Erlang commanded Monkey King. "The Sage Equal to Any in Heaven fears no one!" Monkey King shouted back defiantly.

二郎神騎著飛鷹來到花果山單挑美猴王。美猴王拿著如意金箍棒迎戰，兩人打得風雲變色，日月動搖。二郎神太厲害了！美猴王不敵，只好逃回水簾洞。二郎神追到洞口，大喊：「妖猴，還不快快投降！」美猴王不肯認輸，大聲回喊：「我齊天大聖天不怕、地不怕！」

The monkey then changed into a sparrow and darted away from Erlang. But the great warrior became a hawk and chased after him swiftly. Monkey plunged into the river, becoming a fish, but Erlang turned into a heron and snatched him up in his long beak.

美猴王眼見逃不掉，就變成了一隻麻雀，飛向天空。沒想到二郎神竟然變成老鷹，緊追不捨。美猴王情急之下往河裡衝，變成一條魚，二郎神則變成蒼鷺，尖長的嘴一下就咬住魚的尾巴。

Monkey King then became a cobra snake and whipped Erlang with his tail before disappearing into the grass. The general regained his true form and stunned the cobra with a stone shot from his sling.

Now, for the very first time, Monkey King was injured and could fight no more. He crawled up into the mountains and quickly changed into a pagoda; his body became the walls, his mouth the door, his eyes the windows...and his tail stuck up like a flagpole. When Erlang found the strange building, he wasn't fooled by Monkey King. "Hah! A pagoda never has a flagpole!" He kicked in the door and smashed the windows with his sword, rattling Monkey King's head.

美猴王趕緊變成一條眼鏡蛇，從二郎神的腳跟溜過。當他鑽進草堆時，還用尾巴打了二郎神一下。二郎神恢復原形，用彈弓「啪！」的一聲，狠狠地打中了眼鏡蛇的頭。

美猴王這回真的受傷了，他趕快爬回山裏，變成一座土地廟休息；他的身體變成牆，嘴變成門，眼睛變成窗戶…尾巴豎起來當旗桿。「土地廟有旗桿，真好笑！」二郎神看到這個奇怪的廟，馬上知道是美猴王變的。他一腳踢開了門，接著手起劍落把窗戶搗成碎片，震得美猴王昏頭轉向。

Taking his true shape again, Monkey King was now caught. Luckily the magic buns he had eaten made him feel no pain and the Emperor's potion quickly healed his wounds. General Erlang tied Monkey up in a rope of heavenly silk and hauled him before the Jade Emperor. The Emperor's eyes smoldered. "You have had two chances to prove yourself, but you were too wild, mischievous, and selfish. Now, I'll cook the magic out of you in my white-hot cauldron!"

現出原形的美猴王就這樣被逮住了。幸好他吃的仙餅和仙露
讓他的傷很快就好了。

二郎神用仙索緊緊地捆住美猴王，把他帶到玉皇大帝的面前
。玉皇大帝氣得兩眼昏花：「你曾經有兩次機會學好，但是
你還是那麼蠻橫、調皮、自私。我今天要把你丟進八卦爐，
燒盡你的法力。」

Monkey King just chattered and giggled as he was stuffed into the cauldron that was like a blasting furnace. After forty-nine days, the Jade Emperor finally opened the huge pot, expecting to see only ashes. But there was Monkey King, still jabbering away, still alive thanks to the sacred peaches, the potion, and magic buns. Only his eyes were stinging and red from the smoke, and this sent him jumping about in a rage. He took Ruyi from behind his ear and began smashing everything in Heaven.

八卦爐像個煉鐵爐，熱風滾滾，可是美猴王一點也不怕，還在爐子裡咯咯地笑呢！原來他在天宮偷吃的仙桃、仙餅、仙露已經使他成爲不怕刀、槍、水、火的鐵金剛了。

過了四十九天，玉皇大帝以爲美猴王已被燒成灰燼了，沒想到一掀開爐蓋，美猴王竟神氣活現地跳出來。他揉揉被煙燻紅的眼睛，怒氣大發，從耳朵後面抽出如意金箍棒，在天宮亂打一番。

The gods and goddesses fled in panic as Monkey shattered many beautiful temples and pagodas. The Jade Emperor was now very worried that the awful monkey couldn't be stopped. He sent an urgent message to the great Buddha, who came at once. Buddha smiled at Monkey King, "How can such a tiny earthly monkey cause so much mischief here in Heaven?" Monkey puffed out his chest and announced, "I'm Monkey King, the Heavenly Sage. I've beaten Jade Emperor. Now I will rule his palace."

Buddha's face was serene. "But here you have caused only confusion. It's true you have some great powers, but you're never satisfied with what you have. Do you really think you're wise enough to rule Heaven?" Then Buddha extended his hand. "If you can fly out of my right hand, the palace is yours. But if you can't, you'll be punished. Are we agreed?" Monkey King looked at Buddha's right hand – it was only about the size of a lotus leaf – so he shouted, "Agreed!"

天宮裡牆倒廟塌，諸神眾仙嚇得四處逃命。玉皇大帝真的擔心了，難道沒有人可以管這隻野猴子嗎？他立刻派人去請南海如來佛。如來佛來到天宮，和氣地對美猴王說：「你小小一隻土猴子，怎敢大鬧天宮？」美猴王挺起胸膛得意地說：「我是美猴王，齊天大聖，玉皇大帝是我的手下敗將，現在天宮是我的了。」

如來佛仍然不動氣，他詳和地說：「雖然你法力高強，可是卻不滿足，也不知如何善用這些法力，只會到處搗亂，你真的以為你能治理天宮嗎？」他伸出一隻手，對美猴王說：「如果你能飛出我的手掌心，天宮就是你的；如果飛不出，你就要受罰，好嗎？」美猴王看看如來佛的右手，只有蓮花葉那麼大，於是大喊：「一言為定！」

Monkey King stepped onto Buddha's hand, then he soared up into the clouds. In a flash, he was eighty thousand miles away. He saw five rose-bronze marble pillars rising in the green mist. "Aha!" he thought to himself, "This must be the fence at the sky's end. I'll just leave my mark, then I'll go back to claim my prize." Using a brush made from his own hairs, he wrote on the middle pillar: *Monkey King was here!* Then, to be sure, he peed at the base of the pillar.

Monkey flew back to the Heavenly Palace. "I'm back from the end of the sky," he said. "Now give me the palace!" Buddha smiled, "Can you prove it?"

"Of course! I wrote my name at the end of the sky. Go see for yourself." Buddha held out his right hand. "Is this your handwriting?" Sure enough, on Buddha's middle finger were the characters Monkey had written. And there too was the smell of a monkey!

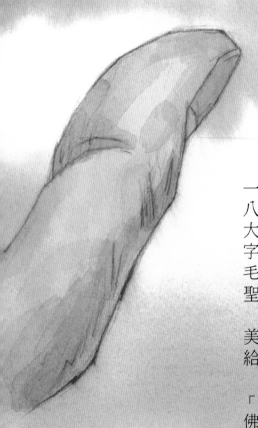

一個筋斗雲，美猴王跳出如來佛的手掌，一飛就飛了八萬哩。在一層薄薄的綠氣中，他看到五根紅褐色的大理石柱。「哈！這一定就是天的盡頭，我來寫幾個字，這樣就可以回去領獎品了。」他從身上拔下一根毛，變出一枝毛筆，在中間的柱子上寫著：「齊天大聖，到此一遊」，還順便在柱子下面撒了一泡尿。

美猴王飛回天宮，對如來佛說：「我回來了，把天宮給我吧！」如來佛笑道：「何以証明？」

「我在天邊的柱子上寫了字，你自己去看看！」如來佛伸出右手：「這是你寫的嗎？」哇！可不是嗎？如來佛的右手中指上，正有「齊天大聖，到此一遊」八個字，甚至還有猴子的尿味呢！

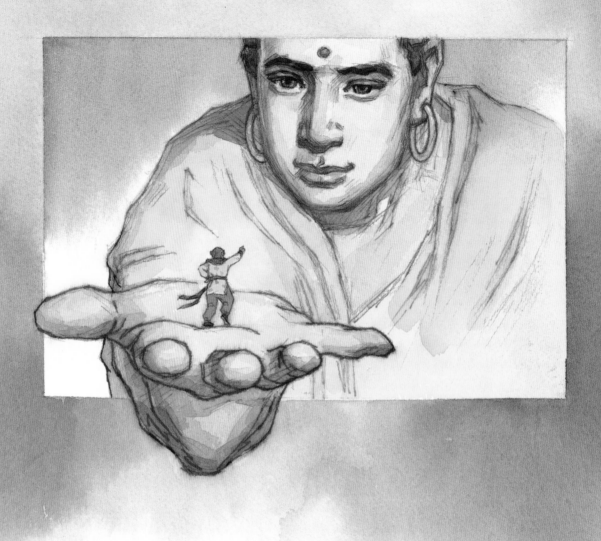

Monkey King tried to run away, but Buddha held him with his right hand. Monkey cried out, "Gentle-hearted Buddha, let me go! I'll be good, I'll change!" Buddha's voice rang like a golden bell, "You used your powers to bring chaos. You were given chances to be good, but you chose to remain wild. Now you must learn or be lost forever."

Buddha pushed Monkey King out of the gates of Heaven. A reflection of Buddha's hand became a five-peaked mountain that pinned Monkey King to the Earth. "You shall stay there for five hundred years," echoed Buddha's voice.

"Five hundred years!" cried Monkey King. "How will I live?"

"Wet your lips with dew. Eat fruits that drop within your reach. I have put a sign at the top of the mountain that tells your story. One day, someone will take the sign down and you will be free again." Monkey King groaned from his cramped space, "Who will ever do that for me?"

"It is a person who is not yet born," said Buddha, his voice fading into the mists of time.

美猴王正要逃，如來佛一把抓住他。「慈悲爲懷的如來佛，請放開我，以後我一定乖乖的！」如來佛用金鐘般宏亮的聲音對他說：「你仗勢欺人，無法無天，有機會也不學好，現在你要接受教訓，否則萬劫不復。」

如來佛把美猴王推出天門，手一翻，五根手指變成一座五行山，把美猴王牢牢地壓在下面。「你就在這兒關個五百年。」如來佛的聲音在山谷中迴響。

「五百年！我怎麼活？」美猴王哭了。

「口渴了，喝露水；肚子餓了，吃樹上掉下來的水果。我在五行山上貼有密帖，上面記載你的故事，有一天，有人會撕去密帖，把你救出來。」「是誰啊？」美猴王從岩縫裏哀哀地問。

「那個人還没有出生呢！」如來佛的聲音遁入渺渺的時空中…